KONDO & KEZUMI

REACH BELL BOTTOM

Written by David Goodner
Illustrated by Andrea Tsurumi

LITTLE, BROWN AND COMPANY
New York   Boston

About This Book

The illustrations for this book were drawn in pencil and rendered digitally. This book was edited by Esther Cajahuaringa and designed by Jenny Kimura. The production was supervised by Virginia Lawther, and the production editor was Annie McDonnell. The text was set in Bembo MT Pro, and the display type is Inagur Pro.

Little, Brown and Company
Hachette Book Group
1290 Avenue of the Americas, New York, NY 10104

Visit us at LBYR.com

First Edition: January 2021

Little, Brown and Company is a division of Hachette Book Group, Inc.
The Little, Brown name and logo are trademarks of Hachette Book Group, Inc.

The publisher is not responsible for websites (or their content) that are not owned by the publisher.

Library of Congress Cataloging-in-Publication Data
Names: Goodner, David, author. | Tsurumi, Andrea, illustrator.
Title: Kondo & Kezumi reach Bell Bottom / written by David Goodner;
illustrated by Andrea Tsurumi.
Other titles: Kondo and Kezumi reach Bell Bottom
Description: First edition. | New York : Little, Brown and Company, 2021. | Series: Kondo & Kezumi; 2 | Audience: Ages 6-10. | Summary: As best friends Kezumi and Kondo continue their exploration, they keep disagreeing about what their next adventure should be but finally remember what matters most—friendship.
Identifiers: LCCN 2020028881 | ISBN 9780759554733 (hardcover)
Subjects: CYAC: Adventure and adventurers—Fiction. | Islands—Fiction. | Best friends—Fiction. | Friendship—Fiction. | Sea stories.
Classification: LCC PZ7.1.G6543 Koj 2021 | DDC [E]—dc23
LC record available at https://lccn.loc.gov/2020028881

ISBN: 978-0-7595-5473-3 (hardcover)

Printed in China

APS

10 9 8 7 6 5 4 3 2 1

To Saphira and Merrick, two people I love even though they're far away — D.G.

For Wendy Forman, with love and poodles — A.T.

I.

To Adventure!

Exploring was exciting. Kondo and Kezumi got to see new places, like an island made of cheese and another made of fire. They met new friends, too, like the island made of Albert.

But sometimes exploring wasn't exciting. Sometimes it was a little sad.

Kondo and Kezumi were a long way from home. Kondo thought about their island with its crooked old trees and crooked old tower. He wondered if the sparkleberry bushes were in bloom, and if the tower needed sweeping. Kezumi thought about home, too, as she searched the clouds for fluffle-bunnies and flitter-birds.

The sea was calm. A gentle breeze blew. Their boat rocked slowly up and down and over the waves.

It was a good day for thinking.

"What are you thinking about?" Kezumi asked.

Kondo thought before he answered. "Cleaning. What are you thinking about?"

"Clouds. That one looks like a flitter-bird. And that one looks like the fluffle-bunny who lives under the sizzlenut tree."

Their sail suddenly fluttered. The breeze puffed into a strong, steady wind.

Kezumi smiled. "To adventure!" she cried as she gripped the tiller.

Kondo flipped over the map. "Which one is Adventure? I thought we were going to Spaghetti Island."

Kezumi sighed. "We ARE going to Spaghetti Island. And when we get there, we're going to have an adventure."

"I hope we have spaghetti. I'm tired of coconuts," said Kondo.

Kezumi was tired of coconuts, too. Kondo had eaten the last of the dried sparkleberries. And the last of the specklenuts. Kezumi didn't say that, though. She said, "We should get to Spaghetti Island tonight or tomorrow morning."

II

To Spaghetti!

Bloop! Their boat jerked.

"Finally," Kondo said. "I miss ground."

"I miss adventure," Kezumi said.

Ba-Bloop! The boat shifted against the waves, against the wind.

"What was that?" Kondo asked.

"Adventure?" Kezumi replied. She looked out toward the *bloops*. She didn't see anything bloopy.

"Adventure is bumpy." Kondo grabbed the mast. "I thought we had hit land."

BA-BLOOP!

The boat lurched and the sail rippled.

"Adventure is dragging us off course," Kezumi said. She saw something. "Kondo! Look!"

"Off course!" Kondo huffed. "What about Spaghetti Island?"

"Kondo, LOOK!"

Kondo looked. There were sea jumpers, lots and lots of sea jumpers. There were so many sea jumpers that they made a powerful path through the water. It pulled Kondo and Kezumi out to the deep ocean. They were dragged left and right and left again— farther and farther they twirled off course.

"Why are they swimming so deep?" Kezumi
wondered. "Where could they be going?"

"Probably to lunch," Kondo groused. With
their boat shaking so much, he couldn't even chop
open a coconut.

Kondo grabbed an oar and held the other one out to Kezumi. "We need to go the other way."

"The other way?" Kezumi ignored the oar. "We need to find out where they're going! It's probably amazing."

Kondo crossed his arms. "Spaghetti Island is probably amazing."

"Spaghetti Island
can be probably
amazing *later.*" Kezumi stamped her foot. "The sea
jumpers are moving *now.* If we don't follow them,
we'll never know where they're going."

"We can ask Albert!" Kondo stamped his foot.
The whole boat rocked.

"But I want to SEE it myself," Kezumi insisted.

"Well, I want to see Spaghetti Island," Kondo
grumped.

"Sea jumpers!" Kezumi started to adjust the sail.

"Spaghetti!" Kondo started to row the other way.

SPLASH!

A pod of sea jumpers leaped over the boat.
They shook it. They spun it.
They soaked it. They almost spilled it.

16

By the time Kondo and Kezumi got the boat
under control, the sea jumpers were far away.

"Phew," Kezumi said. "Are you okay?"

"I lost my coconut," Kondo answered.

The trail of sea jumpers disappeared in the
distance.

"I lost my adventure," Kezumi said.

To...Something Else

The way back to the way to Spaghetti Island was twisty and slippery. Kezumi did her best to steer them on course. Kondo did his best to keep them there. "Watch out!" Kondo said. "There's something in the way."

It was a big something. It was a strange something. They sailed closer.

"It looks a little like a tower," Kezumi said.

Despite himself, Kondo was curious. "It looks rusty. Is there a Rusty Island?"

"There is, but it's way over that way," Kezumi said. She adjusted the tiller.

"What are you doing?" Kondo asked.

"Taking a side trip?"

"Wait, what?!" Kondo demanded.

"Kondo, we found something that's not on the map! We have to go see it."

Kondo crossed his arms. "We have to go see Spaghetti Island."

"We can go there next!" Kezumi said. "It's not even out of the way. That much."

"It's not spaghetti." Kondo could glare almost as big as Kezumi when he wanted to.

"It's new!"

"It's not spaghetti!"

"It's moving."

"It's not spa—

what?"

Kezumi pointed. "If we don't go now, we may never find it again." No one had as sad a sad face as Kezumi. "We'll go to Spaghetti Island right after. I promise."

Kondo sighed a tiny sigh. "Okay. We can stop and look. Just for a little while."

Kezumi clapped. "You don't mind?"

Kondo didn't mind too much.

Soon, their little boat reached the big something.

"Is it an island?" Kondo asked.

"It looks like an island. Kind of. But not really."

The kind-of-but-not-really island crept slowly through the ocean. Kondo helped Kezumi climb up the side. Kezumi tied their boat to a metal railing. Then Kondo crawled carefully after her.

"To adventure!" Kezumi cheered.

"To something," Kondo mumbled.

IV

Kind of Not an Island

"It's kind of NOT an island at all," Kondo said as he looked around.

"Is it a ship?" Kezumi asked.

They stood by the railing. The rusty floor rolled gently beneath their feet. Contraptions lay everywhere. Trees and plants grew out of windows and broken boards and little round holes on the side.

"I've never seen contraptions like these,"
Kezumi said.

"Are they contraptions?" Kondo asked. "I
thought they were doohickeys."

"The little ones are doohickeys," Kezumi said.
"But most of them are contraptions."

"I've never seen trees like these," Kondo said. He was so interested in the trees that he didn't notice Kezumi padding across the creaky deck until she was way far away. "Hey, where are you going?" Kondo yelled.

"To see what else there is."

Kezumi kept going. Kondo followed after her, through a doorway. "Slow down!"

The inside of Kind of Not an Island was dark. Specks of light filtered through the dirty windows. Strange shapes cast scary shadows. Kondo worried it was full of monsters. Kezumi went in. Kondo stayed by the door.

Kezumi ran from thing to thing.

She held up a small, round object. "Look at this! However I turn it, the arrow points the same way!" Kezumi kept running. "And look at this!" She spun a huge wheel. "I bet it steers the ship."

"Should you mess with that?" Kondo edged slowly into the room. He saw a book lying near the wheel. "Maybe there are instructions."

Kondo picked up the book and dusted off the cover. "Captain's Log."

"It's not a log," Kezumi protested. "It's a book."

Kondo rolled his eyes and started reading.

DAY 853

The mission continues. The professor saved most of the samples despite the setback. We will gather more. Someday soon we will understand the secrets of this place.

"Hey, Kezumi, I think they were explorers, like us."

Kezumi's voice came from down a hatch.

"So this IS a boat!"

"Where did you go?" Kondo looked down the dark hatch.

"There's more stuff down here!" Kezumi called.

"It looks scary. The
monsters could be there!"
"Kondo!" Kezumi sighed.

Cautiously, Kondo went
down the stairs. "If there are
monsters, I'm going to be very upset."

V

To Bell's Bottom!

There were no monsters. But there were more contraptions.

Kezumi climbed and crawled and poked around everything. "Look at all this stuff. Isn't it amazing?"

"Amazing," Kondo echoed. But Kondo wasn't watching Kezumi. He was reading the book.

Day 967
   Bell's Bottom damaged the hull. Its danger cannot be underestimated. The professor designed a warning system so it will not happen again.

"That sounds scary," Kondo said.

"I think I found it," Kezumi called out. She was looking down another hatch. Dim blue light glowed from the chamber beyond. Inside was a bell-shaped container with a glass bottom floor. The glass had a huge crack that someone had fixed.

"Found what?" Kondo said as he edged closer.

"Bell's Bottom!"

"What kind of bell is that?" Kondo asked. "It doesn't look like it would ring."

Kezumi slid down the ladder to get a closer look. Kondo didn't even bother to say "Be careful." He just followed after her.

Colorful sea creatures swam through bright corals growing beneath the glass. Kezumi looked up at Kondo. "Someday we could go under there. Below the bell's bottom."

Kondo was entranced. He barely noticed when Kezumi left.

A sea jumper shot through the water.

A sea sinker sank past the glass.

A sea spinner spun around the window.

Then…the sea coral started to creep away! Kondo watched as a hundred little feet scurried across the glass bottom. Through the wiggling of a thousand tiny tentacles, Kondo saw a single eye. The eye saw Kondo, too.

It winked.

Kondo winked back.

"Even if we visit every island there is to visit," Kondo marveled, "we'll never see all there is to see."

The Last Word

Kezumi kept looking. Kondo kept reading.

Day 2006

The professor has left. Or I suppose I have left the professor. She doesn't understand our mission. She wants to study a single island, rather than conduct a full survey. Fine, then. I will continue without her.

The professor sounds annoying, Kondo thought. *If you make a plan, you should stick to it.* Then Kondo thought of Kezumi. *Where is she now?*

He found her on the deck with a pile of stuff.

"Are you ready to go?" she asked.

Kondo threw his hands in the air. "That's not going to fit in the boat."

Before Kezumi could groan, her stomach did.

"Why don't you pick one thing and I'll make lunch?" Kondo said.

Kezumi looked at her pile and at their boat. The pile was bigger than the boat.

"Okay," she said.

Kondo cooked while Kezumi tried to pick her favorite thing. "Are you ready for lunch?" Kondo called out.

"I guess so." Kezumi wished they had a bigger boat.

Day 2099

I regret leaving the professor. I have seen many things, but I have no one to share them with. I fear I will never complete this adventure on my own. Yet what else can I do? I hope someone will find our research and use our tools someday.

"That's so sad," Kezumi said.

"Yeah," Kondo agreed. "We should go."

"To adventure!" Kezumi cried.

"To Spaghetti Island," Kondo grunted.

VII.

Foiled in Fog

They watched as the empty ship drifted away on its long, lonely journey. Kondo wrote on the map:

floaty island

The wind was brisk, even a little chilly. They made good time. "I think we'll still get to Spaghetti Island in the morning," Kezumi said.

That was before a thick fog rolled in and wrapped their boat in a blanket of fuzz.

"Kondo, drop the anchor," Kezumi called.

"What? Why?"

"I can't see."

"But I don't want to stop," Kondo insisted.

"We should wait for the fog to clear."

Kondo didn't want to wait. He'd been waiting.

He was through with waiting. "No," he said.

Kezumi tried to explain. "Kondo…I can't steer."

"You kept the gadget that points the way," Kondo insisted. He almost stamped his foot.

"Well, kind of…," Kezumi said.

"Then let's go. We did all kinds of stuff you wanted to do. Now it's my turn."

Kezumi wanted to say something else, but what she DID say, carefully, was "Okay."

They sailed toward Spaghetti Island. Probably.

VIII.

Not Spaghetti Island

The fog lasted a long time. It was damp and cold. Kondo and Kezumi didn't talk much. There was nothing to hear but the lap of waves against the hull.

And bump

and **THUNK**

and **SCRAPE** when something hit the boat.

45

"What was that?" Kondo cried.

"I don't know!" Kezumi said.

"But there's another one."

They almost hit
something else, too. It was
a floating sign with a tiny bell
that jingled in the wind.

"Kondo, this is really bad. We
need to stop," Kezumi said.

BEWARE BELL'S
BOTTOM

Something spiky stuck out of the water. She
leaned on the tiller to dodge it.

But there was another one.
Kondo pushed with his oar.
"No. You promised."

The water was
rougher around the
spiky things. They were tricky
to see in the fog. Some barely poked
up above the waves. Kezumi had to steer
hard. Kondo had to call out warnings.
Even so, the boat got scraped,
and a part of it broke.

Kondo and Kezumi were soaked and exhausted when they finally washed up on a beach.

"Whew!" Kezumi gasped.

"The boat is broken again," Kondo said.

"It's your fault," Kezumi said. "We shouldn't have tried to sail in the fog." She kicked the broken part, which didn't help anything.

"No, it's YOUR fault," Kondo said. "We shouldn't have gotten lost. Or spent all day looking at old junk. If we'd gone straight, we'd be having spaghetti now!"

"I...It's not...," Kezumi sputtered. She was so mad she couldn't put words together. "That's not right!"

"You're not right," Kondo said. And, even though he knew it wasn't true, he said, "You're never right." Then he stormed off down the beach.

And even though she knew it wasn't true, Kezumi said, "I should have gone without you." Then she stormed down the beach the other way.

IX

Kezumi Can't Fix It

Kezumi stomped so hard her footprints were almost as deep as Kondo's. She grumbled the whole way. "I told him to wait. I told him I couldn't see. He never pays attention."

BANG! Since she wasn't paying attention, she walked right into a post. "Ouch." She kicked it. "OUCH."

The post was connected to a construction, or maybe a contraption. Kezumi explored it, briefly forgetting how mad she was or how much her toe hurt.

It was a tower made of metal. And it was one of the best kinds of things… one that needed fixing. There was an old, dented ladder and an old, cracked roof that had mostly fallen in. And there was a big, round thing down at the bottom.

Kezumi suspected it belonged at the top of the tower. There were broken ropes and rusty brackets. She tapped on it.

It went **ping**.

She hit it harder. It went **bong**.

She hit it with a rock

and it went

BONG!

"It's a bell!" Kezumi
exclaimed. "I wonder why it's here."

But mostly she wondered
if she could fix it.

She climbed up and down, looking for what was broken and how to fix it. Some pieces had fallen off. She put them back. Others had worn away. Where she could, she made new ones with wood and rope.

But one part she couldn't fix, no matter how hard she tried. The bell was just too heavy.

I bet Kondo could do it, she thought.

X.
Kondo Does What He Does Best

Kondo huffed and grumbled as he walked around the beach. "This is all Kezumi's fault."

He trudged and rumbled right into the door of a metal hut. "Ouch," cried Kondo. He wanted to kick the door, but he didn't. Instead, he knocked.

The door creaked open. "Hello?" Kondo said.

"Hello?" a voice answered.

Kondo peeked inside the doorway. The hut had a nice floor and colorful walls. There was a big kitchen with a big stove. Pots and pans hung from the ceiling. Four metal chairs circled a metal table. On one of the four chairs sat a small metal figure.

"Oh, hello!" Kondo said again. "I'm Kondo."

"Hello!" spoke the figure. "I'm B-11."

"B–11?" Kondo repeated.

"Bell for short."

"Bell!" said Kondo, surprised. "Have you ever seen Bell's Bottom?"

"Of course I have," said Bell. "It's right over there." Bell pointed toward the other end of the island. The end of the island where Kezumi was. "It's my job to ring the bell in Bell's Bottom in the fog and in the dark," said Bell. "Except it is broken."

Kondo was confused. "I'm confused."

"About what?" asked Bell.

"About everything." Kondo sighed a sad sigh. Then he told Bell about Kezumi and the map and their adventures and Floaty Island (with its bell bottom!) and Spaghetti Island and the fog and the wreck.

"That is confusing," Bell admitted. "And sad."

Kondo's eyes swelled with tears. He was sad… and mad…and hungry.

"I wish I could cry," Bell said. "It is lonely here without a bell to ring in the fog and in the dark and even in the day—just for fun."

Kondo wiped a tear from his eye. Something rang in his mind. "Bell," he said. "I have an idea." Before Bell could say another word, Kondo cracked open a coconut and started to cook.

XI.
To-GETHER!

Kezumi missed Kondo, even though she was still mad at him. She missed him so much she could almost smell his cooking.

She tried to pull the bell one more time, as
hard as she could. It just barely, maybe, lifted up.
But then the rope slipped out of her hands and it
fell back down.

"UHH!" Kezumi wanted to kick the bell.
Instead, she sat in the sand and very deliberately
did not cry.

A breeze started to blow away the fog. And it carried a scent. Coconuts. Roasted coconuts. It WAS Kondo's cooking.

Kezumi stood up and dusted herself off. There was something more important that needed fixing.

*

Kondo flipped the coconuts and added fruit slices.
His heart flipped and stirred, thinking about
Kezumi. She was probably lonely, too. And it wasn't
really her fault that they weren't on Spaghetti Island.
And it was really kind of HIS fault.

Bell helped Kondo mix everything into one big
bowl.

"Ready?" asked Kondo.

"For what?" asked Bell.

"To go to Bell's Bottom," Kondo said. He pointed to the end of the island. The fog was lifting. Way down on the other side of the island, Kondo could see a tower.

Way closer, Kondo could see Kezumi. Bell saw her, too. "Go," Bell said. "Go see your friend."

Kondo ran toward Kezumi, careful not to spill.

Kezumi hurried toward Kondo,

careful not to fall.

"Hi, Kondo." Kezumi was dusty and dirty and had a skinned knee.

"Hi, Kezumi." Kondo held a bowl of roasted coconut chips and fresh fruit slices.

"Is that food?" Kezumi asked.

Kondo nodded.

"Is that food for me?" she asked.

"Some of it is."

"I was really mad at you," Kezumi said. "But I
also missed you."

"I was pretty mad at you, too," Kondo said.
"You did some things I didn't like. But some of
them weren't your fault. And I missed you, too."

"How do we not be mad?" Kezumi asked.

"I don't know," Kondo said. He handed Kezumi a fork.

"These are really good," Kezumi said.

"I found that fruit on Floaty Island," Kondo said. "I don't want to be like the Captain, without my friend. Or Bell, without my bell. Maybe, sometimes we make each other mad. Like sometimes we get lost in the fog. And we can't change that—"

"But we can change what we do about it,"
Kezumi finished.

"We can," Kondo said. He ate some berries.
"I'm so glad we found something besides coconuts
to eat. Even if it's not spaghetti."

"We can still go find Spaghetti Island," Kezumi
said. "But we need to fix the boat. And there's one
other thing I'd like to fix, if you'll help me."

Kondo knew better than to ask Kezumi to leave something unfixed. And once she showed him what it was, he knew they needed to fix it.

"That bell is to warn boats about the reef," Kondo said. "This is the real Bell's Bottom. But we didn't pay attention. I didn't pay attention."

Kezumi patted him on the knee. "It's okay. We only got banged up a little bit. Then you made dinner."

"And I made a new friend," said Kondo.

"You did!" Bell chimed in.

Before nightfall, Bell and Kondo and Kezumi fixed
Bell's bell and the boat and everything else, too. Together.
BONG! BONG! BONG!

XII.

Noodled Again!

"So, this is Spaghetti Island," Kondo said. "It doesn't smell like spaghetti."

"It looks a little like spaghetti," Kezumi said. "A little."

"I don't think I want to go to Spaghetti Island anymore," Kondo said.

"PHEW!" Kezumi was relieved. She REALLY didn't want to go to Spaghetti Island. She made a note on the map.

← Bring your own Spaghetti!

SPAGHETTI ISLAND

Kondo and Kezumi sailed off and
never argued again. Except when
they did.

THE END (not at all)